The Supply Teacher's Surprise

by

Mirabelle Maslin

Augur Press

THE SUPPLY TEACHER'S SURPRISE
Copyright © Mirabelle Maslin 2010
The moral right of the author has been asserted

Author of:
Beyond the Veil
Tracy
Carl and other writings
Fay
On a Dog Lead
Emily
The Fifth Key
The Candle Flame

British Library Cataloguing in Publication Data.
A catalogue record for this book is available from the British Library.

ISBN 978-0-9558936-4-3

First published 2010 by
Augur Press
Delf House,
52, Penicuik Road,
Roslin,
Midlothian EH25 9LH
United Kingdom

Printed by Lightning Source

The Supply Teacher's Surprise

To all readers who enjoy my writing

Chapter One – The Supply Teacher

Mrs MacLeod had flu. She had started to feel ill at lunchtime on Friday, and in the end she had had to go home.

When the primary six class arrived at school the following Monday morning, they found a supply teacher waiting for them.

'I wonder what she'll be like?' Abby whispered to Nicole.

'She looks okay,' Nicole whispered back. 'But we don't need to worry. It's nearly the end of term.'

It was June, and everyone was looking forward to the summer break.

The supply teacher addressed them. 'Good morning, class. I'm Miss Fairhurst, and I'll be here for the whole of this week.'

'Good morning, Miss Fairhurst,' the class replied politely.

'I have the class list here,' Miss Fairhurst informed them briskly, 'but you'll all have to help me to match the names to the faces.'

As Miss Fairhurst read through the list, Abby stared at her intently. There was something about her that was unusual, but she couldn't work out what it was. She was wearing ordinary clothes – a black skirt, a white blouse with narrow cream stripes on it, and a pair of flattish black shoes. She wasn't young, and she wasn't old. She had a pair of stylish glasses hanging round her neck on a fine metal chain. She wasn't tall and she wasn't small, and she had brown curly hair.

Then Abby suddenly realised what it was. 'Got it!' she murmured.

Nicole nudged her. 'What?' she whispered.

'Tell you at break,' Abby replied.

It was that hairstyle. There was nothing wrong with it, but it reminded Abby of some pictures out of a very old magazine that she had found at her granny's. It wasn't remarkable that Miss Fairhurst

1

had curly hair. It was the way that her hair was curled, and how the curls were arranged, that was unusual. She wondered if Nicole had noticed the same thing, but she made no attempt to speak to her, as they were getting ready for a maths lesson.

By the time break came, there was more to talk about than curly hair. Miss Fairhurst could never be as good as Mrs MacLeod, but she was great! She was picking up all their names really quickly, and for Abby, maths had suddenly taken on an extra meaning. Plenty of the rest of the class were finding the same, and there was much chatter about what would come next.

It was after lunch on Wednesday that the big surprise came. Miss Fairhurst had announced that morning that she was going to talk to them about an idea she'd had. They all sat round their tables, waiting expectantly.

Stephen shuffled his feet noisily.

'Sh!' said Emma. Stephen was sitting next to her, and she didn't want his wriggling to spoil things.

Miss Fairhurst began. 'I want to talk to you about a young friend of mine who's doing a project at university.'

Mark groaned audibly. He was fed up of hearing about university. His big brother was going there after the summer, and the way his mum and dad were going on, you would have thought he'd won the Lottery.

Laura dug him in the ribs with her elbow. 'Shut up!' she hissed.

Miss Fairhurst smiled. 'I'm going to talk to you about projects. You've got the whole summer holiday ahead of you. My friend has to do a project for her university course this summer, and I've been thinking about things I could suggest to all of you.'

Diane sat on the edge of her chair. She was interested... very interested. She and her family couldn't go away on holiday this year because her big cousin had just had a baby, and they were all going to help her to look after him. She guessed that her mum wouldn't be able to put baby Gary down, so she wouldn't get much of a look in, and the idea of a project of her own appealed to her. She listened while Miss Fairhurst continued.

'I'll tell you the kind of things I had in mind, and you can tell me what you think. After that, we could add more ideas to the list. And remember, no one *has* to do a project.'

'Good!' said Chloe rudely.

Emma stared at her, shocked. Not only was it a really bad thing to say, but also it was not like Chloe to speak like that.

'Is something the matter, Chloe?' asked Miss Fairhurst kindly.

Chloe hung her head, and Emma could see her cheeks going red. Chloe mumbled something, but no one could make out what she said.

'You can tell me later if you want,' said Miss Fairhurst, before continuing. 'Now, the first thing I want to say is that it's good to do projects in groups.'

'But we can't,' Dylan objected. 'I'm going to be away for nearly the whole of the holiday, so I won't be seeing anybody.'

'Me too,' said Jack.

'That doesn't have to be a problem,' Miss Fairhurst explained cheerfully. 'There are plenty of projects where people can gather information and then share it.'

Dylan and Jack looked pleased.

'Why don't I tell you what's on my list so far?' Miss Fairhurst suggested. She took out a small notebook, and read from it. 'World War Two, wild plants, where our food comes from, healthy exercise, and making up a play.'

'The primary sevens always do a World War Two project,' said Julie quickly. 'My sister did it last year before she went to High School.'

'Yes, that's right,' Miss Fairhurst replied. 'You'll be doing it, and you'll enjoy it more if you've done your own research first.'

Research. Julie liked the sound of that word. Yes, this was something she could see herself doing. For a start, she knew that her gran had a lot of old photos in a box in the attic, and she would ask if she could have a look through them. And in P7 she would definitely make a better job of the project than her sister had.

'My food comes from the supermarket,' said Cameron, grinning.

'Do you think some of it grows there in cardboard boxes?' asked Miss Fairhurst calmly.

'Nah!' Cameron replied.

Miss Fairhurst went on. 'Some of you might be interested to list the items on the ingredients panel of boxed meals, and then work out what they are and where they come from. It would be quite a challenge, because some of the ingredients are tricky to trace.'

To the surprise of the class, Cameron volunteered straight way. 'Just the job for me!'

'Good,' Miss Fairhurst encouraged. She continued. 'Then there are the fresh foods.'

'I've seen labels on packs of lettuce that tell you who grew it as well as where it was grown,' said Kaitlin seriously.

'That's right,' replied Miss Fairhurst. 'There's produce from the UK, and produce from abroad, and the labels usually only give the country of origin, but recently I've seen the grower's name is sometimes there too.'

Megan put up her hand. 'We could get a big map of the world,' she burst out enthusiastically. 'My dad could make a board for it to go on, and we could get coloured pins to show where things come from.'

'That's an excellent idea, Megan,' Miss Fairhurst approved. 'Are there any more of you who would like to do that project?'

Four hands shot up.

'I'll make a note,' said Miss Fairhurst. 'Megan, Cameron, Usman, Mark and Nicole.'

'I want to try inventing an exercise programme,' said Sam determinedly. 'Dad's taken me to some great activities, but we can't go very often to the ones I like most of all.'

'What do you like best, Sam?' asked Miss Fairhurst.

Sam's face shone. 'The climbing wall near Edinburgh,' he said without hesitation. 'It's brilliant!'

'Sam, I like your idea of an exercise programme,' Stephen told him. 'I'd like to be in your group.'

'And me,' said Shona. 'I'll ask my mum and dad if they'll help.'

4

'Why?' asked Stephen. 'We don't need them.'

'If we get some adults to help, we might be able to use our project to raise some money for charity,' Shona replied.

'Hey, that's good idea!' exclaimed Sam. 'Anyone else for my group?'

'Put my name down, Miss Fairhurst,' said Shannon. 'I've just got a new bike. There's got to be room in the project for that!'

Miss Fairhurst smiled. 'That's all the names in the class beginning with "S".'

Sam was pleased. 'That's cool.'

'If we're going ahead with all of this, we should maybe have the same number of people in each group,' Miss Fairhurst advised. 'We've got twenty-four in the class.'

Andrew had appeared uninterested until now, but he suddenly came to life. 'Five projects. Five people for each, except one. I'm not up for the exercise, but I fancy World War Two.'

'My name doesn't begin with "S",' said Emma suddenly, 'but I really want to do the exercise project.'

'That's fine,' said Sam, Stephen, Shannon and Shona all at the same time. Then they looked at one another and giggled.

' "E" is for exercise,' Sam pointed out. 'You'll definitely fit in.'

'I want to do a play,' said Diane shyly. 'I'm going to be at home all of the summer, so I'd have plenty of time.'

'I'm going to be at home, too,' said Lucy. 'We could do it together.'

'We'd need more people,' Diane pointed out. 'Chloe, are you going to be around?'

Chloe cheered up immediately. She had three big brothers who were always doing things together and leaving her out. To make it worse, her brothers were all going camping that summer with Dad, leaving her behind with Mum to look after their two cats.

'Is anyone else going to be at home all summer?' asked Diane.

Mason surprised them all by saying, 'I am, and I've got some ideas about what the play might be about.'

'What sort of ideas?' asked Lucy.

'Um…' said Mason.

'I think you haven't got any really,' said Lucy unkindly.

Mason was indignant. 'I have! They're about helping.'

'What do you mean "helping"?' asked Diane.

But Mason would not be drawn. 'You'll see,' he said mysteriously. 'I'll write some lines,' he added importantly.

'We'll have to write some as well, but you can start first,' said Diane generously.

'I'm only going to be away for one weekend,' said Laura. 'And I think my mum would help with costumes if we did a play.'

'That's great!' Diane exclaimed. 'A weekend doesn't really count as going away.'

'I'm beginning to wish that I wasn't going away on holiday,' said Abby. 'The play project sounds really exciting. Maybe I could ask Mum if I could stay at Gran's while everybody else goes away.'

'I know what you mean,' said Michelle. 'I'd like to do the play, too, but I think I'd miss my holiday away if I stayed at home while my family went off.'

'Anyway, we've already got five for our group,' Diane reminded them firmly. She felt very strongly that their group was only for people who hadn't got a choice but to be at home.

'I've been thinking…' said Holly slowly. 'I don't want to do anything about World War Two, but I like the idea of a project.'

'Don't worry about World War Two, because I can be doing some of that while I'm away,' Jack announced. 'We're going to stay with my mum's auntie and uncle for the summer. They've got a big house, and there's plenty of room for everyone. They like having us there. They're quite old. I'll find out what they know, and see if they've got friends I could talk to. I could interview them,' he finished confidently.

'Well,' said Miss Fairhurst, 'it looks as if most of you have made a decision already, but do remember to check with your parents about any plans that you make.'

'I don't want to be left out.' Holly sounded quite panicky.

'We can do something together,' Kaitlin reassured her. 'I

haven't decided on anything yet. When are you going to be away?'

'The first two weeks of the holidays,' Holly replied.

'Perfect!' said Kaitlin. 'That's when I'm away too.'

'I'm away for the second week and a few days after that,' said Michelle. 'What shall we do?'

Kaitlin put her finger to her lips. 'It's going to be a secret.'

Miss Fairhurst smiled. 'Then the others will get a surprise when you all come back to school.'

Kaitlin nodded. She hadn't a clue yet as to what their project would be, but she was determined that it would be a good one.

Miss Fairhurst looked at her watch. 'It's time to carry on with our work.'

Ryan looked agitated. 'But what about the rest of us?' he burst out. 'We haven't all got a group yet.'

'Don't worry, Ryan. We can keep some time on Friday free for further discussion,' Miss Fairhurst promised. 'Holly's group might like to tell us what they have decided, and if there's any other news about projects, we'll hear it then.'

Ryan relaxed, and Miss Fairhurst began the next lesson.

At the end of the day everyone gathered in the playground for a while.

'I think we should get the groups properly sorted out,' Ryan announced. 'I've decided to join Jack, Julie and Andrew doing World War Two, but that still leaves Dylan and Abby.'

'I'm in with you, Ryan,' Dylan informed him.

Holly noticed that Abby was looking downcast. She nudged Kaitlin and grabbed Michelle's elbow, saying, 'Abby, we want you in our group.'

'That's right,' Kaitlin agreed, and Michelle nodded vigorously.

Abby cheered up straight away. 'I'll ask Mum if we can have a sleepover as soon as you're back from your holidays, and we can make plans. We're not going away until the last week of the holidays, so we'll have loads of time.'

7

The following morning, Mr Burridge, the school janitor, was very surprised to see what looked like the whole of P6 arriving before any of the other pupils, dividing up into a number of groups, and talking animatedly. At break he observed much the same thing, although it was more difficult to see them as they were partially concealed by the hubbub of everyone else. Curious, he made sure that he was in the playground after lunch, on the pretext of checking round the school fences. Again, he saw the same thing happening. Fleetingly he wondered if they were up to no good, but quickly dismissed the thought, as they made no attempt to conceal what they were doing. They appeared to be oblivious of everything but their conversations. He noticed that some of them had notebooks, and were scribbling in them.

After school, he made a point of going to a window that overlooked the playground to check if anyone was hanging about, but by then there was no one to be seen.

'Strange,' he muttered to himself. 'I could have sworn there's something afoot.' He wondered if he should speak to Mrs Molloy, the head teacher, about what he had seen, but thought better of it, and instead went to have a word with the cleaners. He made a mental note to arrive early the following morning to keep a close eye on things.

'Good morning, class,' Miss Fairhurst greeted them all on Friday morning as they filed into the room and took their seats round the tables.

'Good morning, Miss Fairhurst,' they replied together.

There was an air of barely suppressed excitement.

Miss Fairhurst smiled. 'I can see that you're all bursting to tell me your news. We must finish off yesterday afternoon's piece of work first, but we should have plenty of time to talk after break.'

The class worked quietly and diligently. No one wanted to risk losing any of the precious project-discussion time.

After break they all returned to the classroom promptly, and waited for Miss Fairhurst to return.

Usman was sitting near the door, and he caught sight of her coming down the corridor carrying a substantial cardboard box. Her shoulder bag had slipped onto her arm and was banging against her legs. He jumped up and walked briskly to meet her.

'Can I carry that for you?' he asked politely.

'Thank you, Usman,' she replied. 'That would be a great help.'

Usman was strong. He carried the box with ease, and placed it carefully on the teacher's table. He noticed that it was heavier than he had expected, and he wondered what was inside it.

Miss Fairhurst put her bag down on the table and patted the top of the box.

'I expect you're all wondering what's in here,' she said, smiling. 'Well, I'll begin by letting you know straight way.' She opened the box, and took out a jotter with a brightly coloured cover. 'There's one for each of you,' she explained. 'I thought you'd like to have something you could write in about your projects.'

'I haven't got any money with me,' Chloe said anxiously.

'Don't worry,' Miss Fairhurst reassured her. 'The jotters are a present from me.'

'Wow!' said Ryan.

'Thank you very much, Miss Fairhurst,' said six of the girls together.

Everyone else was either sitting up straight, or turning to their neighbour to say how great Miss Fairhurst was.

Miss Fairhurst beamed at them. 'You deserve them. I know you've been very busy since Wednesday, and I think you're going to make good use of them. I chose five different colours – one for each project.' She looked round the class. 'Ah, I see you're already sitting in your special groups. Will you choose a spokesperson for each?'

There was a babble of voices for a few minutes.

'Right,' Miss Fairhurst went on briskly, 'spokespeople come and collect the jotters and hand them to your group members. Green for food, red for World War Two, pink for the secret, blue for exercise and purple for the play.'

Sam, Laura, Megan, Jack and Abby stood up and took it in turn to collect the jotters.

Miss Fairhurst continued. 'Perhaps you'd all like to take a few minutes to make sure your spokespeople have a note of everything you want to tell us.'

Five minutes later she looked at her watch. 'Can we start with you, Sam?' she asked.

Sam stood up. 'My dad's offered to help us,' he informed the class proudly. 'He'll be our sports advisor, and we think that Shona's mum and dad will teach us about fundraising and sponsoring.'

The class clapped. Sam flushed, smiled, and then sat down.

Miss Fairhurst turned to Laura. 'Would you like to speak next?' she asked.

'My mum was really pleased when I asked her about costumes,' Laura began. 'She's good at sewing, and she said we can look in some charity shops together once we've decided more about the play. Lucy's mum has got a friend who has done amateur dramatics, and she's going to ask if she'll come and talk to us. Mason's written some lines already, but he won't tell us the story yet.' She yelped when Mason stood hard on her foot under the table. She glared at him. 'Well, it's true.'

Mason looked at her darkly. 'I said I'd tell you soon.'

Miss Fairhurst intervened. 'A play is quite a challenging project, so it would be a good idea to share all the information right from the beginning.'

Laura looked at Mason again and hissed, 'See.'

'Okay,' Mason conceded. 'I just wanted time to develop the plot first, but I'll do what Miss Fairhurst says.'

'Jack?' said Miss Fairhurst.

Jack stood up. 'There's not much to report. We've worked out how to keep in touch with each other over the holidays, and we're going to get together at my house every day in the last week. There's a chance that Dylan's dad might be able to take him to the Imperial War Museum, but we're not sure yet.'

'Thank you, Jack,' said Miss Fairhurst. 'Megan?'

'My dad's promised to do the board and make sure we've got a good map of the world to put on it,' Megan reported eagerly. 'We're all going to collect information from labels from food packaging, and then decide exactly what to do. Our first meeting will be at Cameron's house in about two weeks' time.'

Abby's face was covered in a huge grin. She could hardly wait for her turn to speak. Miss Fairhurst nodded to her and she burst out, 'My mum's said that Kaitlin, Michelle and Holly can come and stay for a *whole weekend* after they're back from their holidays, so that we can get our project properly organised.' She sat down again.

'But you haven't told us what your project is,' Stephen complained.

Abby wrinkled up her nose. 'It's a *secret*, silly.'

'That's not fair!' said several of the class crossly, all at the same time.

Abby looked at Miss Fairhurst for support.

Miss Fairhurst addressed them. 'I know it can be frustrating having to wait to find out, but I think we have to respect that group's decision. After all, there are big parts of each project that no one knows about yet.'

The class found this explanation easy to accept, and Stephen found himself saying, 'I'll look forward to your surprise next term.'

'And now I have some news for you all,' said Miss Fairhurst. The class immediately fell silent. 'I've spoken to Mrs Molloy to see if I can visit you next term to hear about the results of your endeavours, and she's agreed.'

'Hooray!' shouted Cameron, and then he clapped his hand to his mouth.

'I like your enthusiasm, Cameron,' said Miss Fairhurst with a twinkle in her eye, 'but we must all remember that shouting can disturb other classes.' She looked round the class and cleared her throat, and Chloe thought for a moment that she looked a little upset. Then Miss Fairhurst continued. 'I want to tell you how much I've enjoyed this week with you.' She picked up her bag and took out a small book. 'I'm going to finish off the morning by reading to you from this collection of short stories. I have chosen one that I think you will all like.'

She had chosen well, because almost as soon as she began to read, the class became completely absorbed in the fascinating tale.

Chapter Two – The Play Project

Diane, Lucy, Chloe, Mason and Laura met together in the park as soon as term ended. It was a warm sunny day, and they settled themselves under a tree, not far from the swings. Each had brought the purple jotter that Miss Fairhurst had given them.

'I think we should meet every day to begin with,' said Mason.

'Yes,' agreed Lucy, 'there's lots to do. My mum's friend Christine says there's always more to do for a play than you would ever imagine.'

'And that's for people who aren't having to write the play first,' added Laura.

'Mason, you'd better tell us how far you've got,' said Diane.

Chloe nodded. 'But before he starts I've got to tell you that Mum says we can meet at my house on rainy days while my brothers are away.'

'That's great!' said Laura. 'It means we'll be able to get on quicker.'

Mason cleared his throat and opened his jotter. Lucy could see that the first page was covered in writing. She was impressed.

'I haven't got a title for the play yet,' Mason began, 'but...'

Here Chloe interrupted excitedly. 'I want to tell you something else first,' she announced. 'Mum told me I'm not supposed to say anything yet, but I'm going to. Well... if you promise not to say anything,' she added hurriedly.

''Course we won't,' Diane assured her. 'Tell.'

The others nodded vigorously, and leaned forward.

Chloe lowered her voice. 'Mum said that if we behave okay, she might let us have a couple of sleepovers.'

'Wow!' said Diane. 'I hope it rains soon, and then she'll see how good we can be at your house.'

'She says we can use the conservatory,' Chloe informed them proudly. 'She's going to take most of the stuff out of it so we'll have more room.' She giggled. 'I'm beginning to feel glad that my dad and my brothers have gone away. I'm going to have a great time without them!'

Laura turned to Mason. 'Okay, you can start now. Never mind about a title, we can make one up later.'

Mason consulted his jotter. 'My idea won't need much in the way of costumes,' he began.

'Oh no!' Laura burst out. 'I was looking forward to doing some with my mum.'

'Don't worry,' Mason reassured her. 'There's one person who'll have to be dressed up and have make-up on and all that sort of thing.'

Laura relaxed and Mason continued.

'A group of children...'

'Us,' stated Lucy.

'... are walking along the road by the shops. It's the summer holiday, and they're on their way to the swimming pool.'

'That's a good idea,' said Chloe, 'but how can we have a swimming pool in my house?'

'We don't, silly.' Mason was clearly annoyed. 'Let me tell you the whole thing, and don't butt in again.'

Chloe's face coloured. She felt squashed, and she said nothing else.

Mason continued. 'They're talking to each other about swimming, when suddenly they see that there's an old person in difficulty. The footpath has been dug up, and there's a bit of the road fenced off instead. The old person has one of those push-along trolley things to help him to walk, and he can't manoeuvre it off the pavement on to the road.'

'So we help,' said Diane brightly. 'His wheely thing is loaded up with some shopping bags, so two of us carry them, and two of us help him with the wheely thing. I like that idea.'

'I hadn't got it all worked out like that,' Mason admitted. He flushed, and quickly began to make notes.

'It's all right,' said Lucy. 'We're supposed to be doing it together anyway. What bit had you done?'

'Hang on a minute. I've got to finish writing this down first,' Mason replied.

Diane nudged Chloe. 'We could be the ones who take the bags.'

Chloe cheered up. 'I'd like that.'

'And me and Laura can help with the wheely thing,' said Lucy.

By this time, Mason had finished writing. 'So that means I'll be the old person.' He thought about it for a minute, and then added, 'Good. Now, let me tell you what else I've got.' The others fell silent, and he continued. 'I've got some lines for offering to help, and a few lines for how the story goes on.'

Lucy was impressed. 'You mean you've got another scene afterwards?'

'Yes,' said Mason proudly, '*and* I have an idea for one after that.'

'*Three* scenes!' exclaimed Laura. 'Just wait until I tell Mum.'

'And I'll tell Christine,' added Lucy quickly.

Mason looked at his jotter. 'Scene two. We walk along with the old person to his house because his legs are feeling wobbly with the stress about the pavement. We chat to him along the way to help him to feel better. Scene three. He invites us in for a while, and he tells us all sorts of interesting things about when he was young. He even tells us a bit about World War Two.'

'Mm,' reflected Lucy, 'Jack's group might not be very pleased about that. We might have to leave it out.'

'I hadn't thought about that,' Mason admitted. 'You could be right.'

'Shall we have it that they go to the swimming pool afterwards?' asked Laura.

'I don't see why we can't,' said Lucy. She turned to Mason. 'What do you think?'

'We could just say something at the end,' he suggested. 'There'll be no need for anything else.'

'We would have to carry swimming things right from the

beginning,' Lucy pointed out.

'So it would be easy to talk about swimming at the end,' Laura finished for her.

'I'll put swimming things in the list of props we'll need,' said Mason.

'Er... what are props?' asked Chloe uncertainly.

'They're things we need for the play, as well as people and costumes,' Mason explained.

'Oh... thanks,' said Chloe. She had heard the word before, but had never been sure what it meant, and for some reason she had never been able to ask. She wished that she was more confident about asking things. Her brothers did not seem to have any difficulty. In fact, they were always asking about things – quite loudly. If she asked them to explain things to her they sometimes helped, but sometimes they were unkind and teased her for not knowing. This meant that she had felt a bit hurt when Mason had called her silly. Mum and Dad were usually so busy that there was never a good time to ask them questions. When she did, they often looked as if they had not heard her, and she did not like to try again. It had felt really nice that Mason had explained about props like he did. This whole play project was beginning to work out really well. Mum was very interested, and she was helping lots by promising that they could use the conservatory. So now, instead of feeling left out since her brothers and her dad went away, she was beginning to feel that she and Mum had something special together. And here she was with a group of friends, *and* Mason was helping her. Maybe he had just been feeling stressed before. She began to think that the play was going to mean a lot more than helping a fictitious old man...

'Can we go through the lines you've written so far?' she burst out enthusiastically.

Mason looked very pleased, and did not wait for any encouragement from the others. 'Scene one. Four girls are walking along the pavement carrying their swimming things, when they notice an old man in trouble. Girl one says...'

Lucy interrupted. 'Sorry to stop you, but can we decide which of us is girl one?'

Chloe was very excited. 'Can I be?' she begged.

Laura, Lucy and Diane agreed immediately.

'You can each have the same number of lines,' Mason told them.

'I'll be girl two,' Diane offered.

'I can be girl three and you can be girl four, Lucy,' said Laura.

Mason continued. 'Girl one… I mean Chloe… says to Diane, "Look, there's an old man in trouble. Let's help." Then Diane says, "Yes, we must." They walk up to him quickly and say together "Excuse me. Can we help?" The old man – that's going to be me – says "I'm fine… No, actually, I'm not. Please can you help me?" Then Chloe and Diane say, "We've got some friends with us, and we can all help you." The old man says, "Thanks very much, but I don't know what to do." Girl three, Laura, says, "Don't worry, two of us can take the heavy shopping off your walking thing, and the other two can help you to steer down off the kerb and along this bumpy bit of road in the gutter." '

Lucy was impressed. 'Mason, that's really really good.'

'I've got a worry,' said Laura.

'What's that?' asked Diane.

'We haven't got a wheely thing, and I can't imagine how we could make one.'

Mason surprised them by saying, 'I've got that all worked out. My gran's got one, and she doesn't use it very often, so I asked if we could borrow it a few times.' He grinned. 'She wanted to know why, but I didn't tell her.'

Lucy looked worried. 'I don't think that's fair.'

Mason went on. 'I promised I wouldn't damage it, and that she would get a nice surprise at the end of the holidays. She was okay about it after that.'

'Yes, we could do our play for her,' said Laura, 'and we won't need her wheely thing for most of our rehearsing. Mason, what do you want to wear for your costume?'

Mason thought for a moment. 'I'll need a jacket, and probably some kind of hat. Does anyone have any ideas?'

'I'll talk to Mum about it,' said Laura. 'I think that we can come up with the right kind of thing.'

'I'd like to go through what Mason's read out so far,' said Lucy. 'I want to see what it feels like.'

'Good idea,' replied Laura. She stood up. 'Come on everyone.'

But just then a football seemed to come out of nowhere, and it crashed into the middle of their group.

'Yow!' shouted Mason as it bounced off his arm. He looked up and saw a group of people approaching. He didn't like the look of them. 'Come on,' he hissed, shutting his jotter quickly. 'Let's go. Head for the gates.'

The girls didn't argue. They walked briskly in the direction of the gates, while Mason put down his jotter and collected the football, preparing to kick it to the approaching group. But one of them ran up and wrenched the ball from him aggressively.

Mason felt very angry, but tried hard to appear casual. 'Hi,' he said. 'Have a good game.' By now he had recognised this person as Seth, the nasty older brother of someone he knew in the next street from where he lived.

He picked up his jotter and turned to leave, but Seth grabbed his arm and said threateningly, 'What were you playing at?'

Mason chose to react as if Seth had been asking what his group had been doing. 'Homework,' he stated. 'Late.'

Seth smirked, and was about to say something else, when the rest of his group shouted across to him to hurry up, and he left.

Mason found the others waiting for him behind a hedge outside the main gate to the park.

'That was *horrible!*' said Lucy angrily. 'We need somewhere more private. I'm going to ask Mum if we can be in our garden. Come on. She'll be at home now. Let's go and ask.'

Ten minutes later she disappeared inside her house, while the others waited inside the gate. It was not long before her mother appeared at the front door.

'Just go round the back,' she called. 'Lucy will open the shed, and you can get the garden chairs out. There's a folding table, too.

You're welcome to use them any time.'

They were soon settled in the middle of the small patch of grass.

'That's better,' said Lucy. 'Now, where were we? Oh, by the way, Mum spoke to her friend Christine. She wanted to help us, but she's going to be away, and then she's got people staying. But she says she hopes our project goes well.'

The days passed quickly as the five planned their play. They met nearly every day. They continued to gather in Lucy's garden when the weather was good, and when it was bad they met in Chloe's conservatory.

After three weeks, they had added a lot to their lines, created Mason's costume, and collected together most of the props. Each time they rehearsed, their performance became more confident, and they expanded and embellished the story. Chloe's mum soon began to look forward to rainy days, as she enjoyed having them in the conservatory. They had one sleepover at the end of the second week, and they would have another one fairly soon, as they were going to prepare to have a dress rehearsal, with Mason's granny as the audience.

One morning, when Laura went to the local supermarket to get a loaf of bread for her mum, she bumped into Kaitlin. They were pleased to see each other.

'How's your secret project going?' Laura asked.

Kaitlin smiled. 'We're about to have our first meeting. We have less than three weeks before Abby goes away, so we'll have to work hard on it. How's your play?'

'It's coming on really well,' Laura replied. 'I can't tell you anything else though, because we want it to be a surprise.'

'Will we all get to see it?' asked Kaitlin.

Laura was uncertain. 'We're going to do it for Mason's granny. I'll have to talk to the others.'

Kaitin put down her basket. 'It's really heavy. I wish I'd taken a trolley, and I don't know how I'm going to get all this home.'

'I can walk round that way with you if you want,' Laura offered.

'I've only come for a loaf of bread, so I can help you to carry things.'

'Thanks,' replied Kaitlin. 'My auntie is staying while Mum's at work, but she was sick this morning, and so she's resting in bed. That's why I'm having to do this on my own.'

On the way down the road, Kaitlin told Laura a little about her holiday. Laura found that she did not feel envious at all, as the past weeks had been full of fun for her.

As they parted at the gate of her house, Kaitlin said, 'I'll be seeing Holly, Abby and Michelle this afternoon. I'll tell them I bumped into you.'

'I hope you have as good a time as we've been having,' Laura replied cheerfully.

At her next meeting with Mason, Chloe, Lucy and Diane, Laura told them of her conversation with Kaitlin. 'Do you think Mrs Molloy would let us do our play for the class when Miss Fairhurst visits?' she finished.

'That's a great idea!' replied Mason excitedly. 'We must ask our teacher when we go back to school.'

'Yes, definitely,' said Diane and Chloe together.

'We don't know who we're getting yet,' Lucy pointed out.

'There won't be a problem,' said Mason confidently. 'If Mrs Molloy is fixing for Miss Fairhurst to come, she's bound to say it's all right for us to do our play.'

Chapter Three – The 'Secret' Project

'I've been thinking about our secret project all the time I've been away,' said Holly. 'My family kept asking me why I wasn't talking as much as usual. I just said I was relaxing, but they didn't believe me.'

Michelle giggled. 'The same thing was happening to me.'

'It was okay for me,' said Kaitlin. 'I was really lucky that I got to do a lot of pony trekking, so I had loads of time to think without anyone noticing.'

'And I've been counting the days till you all came back,' Abby told them. 'It seemed a very long time. But thanks for the postcards you sent – they really helped.' She took her pink jotter out of her bag. 'I'm ready,' she announced in a businesslike way.

They were all sitting clustered on the floor in the living room of Kaitlin's house.

Abby took a pen out of her bag. 'I'll write down everyone's ideas,' she informed them. She turned to Holly. 'You first.'

'It's all very well having a secret project,' Holly began, 'but when you try to think what it might be, it's not so easy. I thought we'd work something out when we got together.'

Michelle nodded. 'That's what it's been like for me, too,' she admitted.

'I hope you all like my idea.' Kaitlin was obviously bursting to tell the others, and could barely contain herself any longer.

'Go on,' said Abby, her pen poised.

'Pets,' Kaitlin announced excitedly. 'We could do how to look after pets.'

'That's a really good idea!' exclaimed Holly.

Kaitlin put her finger to her lips. 'Shush!' she whispered. 'You mustn't wake my auntie up.'

Holly's hand flew to her mouth. 'Oh, no,' she said quietly. 'I'm sorry. I promise I won't forget again.'

Michelle looked thoughtful. 'I'm sure I heard Dad talking about someone who was starting up a dog training business. I'll check.'

'I hope it's someone nice,' said Abby, making a note of this. 'If it is, maybe we could ask if we could interview them.'

Holly looked at her approvingly. 'That's a great idea. Can you find out?'

'I'll ask Dad more about it tonight,' Michelle promised.

'We could start writing out some interview questions,' Abby suggested.

Kaitlin stood up and started rummaging through a heap of magazines and newspapers.

'What are you doing?' asked Abby.

'I'm sure there's something here,' Kaitlin murmured as she searched.

'What?' asked Holly.

'I'm looking for a leaflet,' Kaitlin explained.

'We can help,' Abby offered. 'What is it about?'

Kaitlin began to pass round small heaps from the pile. 'I'm sure a leaflet came before we went away. It might still be here.'

'A leaflet about *what*?' Abby repeated. She sounded exasperated.

'Dog walking, and things like that,' said Kaitlin.

'Is this it?' asked Michelle, holding up a simple leaflet in black and white.

Kaitlin took it. 'Yes, this is it. These people visit dogs and cats when their owners are at work. They help to look after horses, too.'

She passed the leaflet to Abby, who made a few notes in her jotter.

'This sounds really nice,' Abby commented as she wrote. 'They don't just give the animals food, they give them cuddles as well.'

Michelle and Holly took the leaflet and studied it together.

'And they'll look after the pet owner's house,' Holly reported.

Kaitlin looked unhappy. 'I don't like the idea of a pet being left for more than a day,' she stated.

'But if it has to be, then these look like the sort of people who would really help,' Michelle pointed out.

'It's much better if you've got a friend who will take your pet while you're away on holiday,' said Abby. 'Our next-door neighbours are going to feed our rabbits while we're away.'

'Maybe there are people who don't have nice friends or neighbours,' Holly suggested. She consulted the leaflet again. 'I'm looking to see if there's an address,' she explained. 'Here it is!'

Kaitlin stared at her, annoyed. 'Sh!' she hissed. 'My auntie's got to sleep.'

Holly's cheeks turned pink. 'I'm *so* sorry. I didn't mean to,' she whispered.

'Okay,' Kaitlin acknowledged. 'Now tell us where the leaflet's from.'

'It's from Stoneyhill,' Holly replied.

'Where's that?' asked Abby blankly.

'Um... I think it's a village quite near here,' replied Holly uncertainly. Just then she turned to the back of the leaflet. 'Hey! There's a map here,' she added in a low voice.

Kaitlin took it from her and examined the map. But she could not make any sense of it, and tried to hide her confusion by turning it upside down and tracing one of the roads on it with her finger.

'Let me help,' offered Michelle.

Relieved, Kaitlin handed it to her.

'Mm... It looks as if it's too far for us to go on our own,' Michelle began. 'But it's not all that far away.'

'I could ask my mum if she can take us when you come for the weekend to my house,' suggested Abby suddenly.

Kaitlin brightened. 'Do you think she might?'

Abby nodded her head vigorously.

'Wouldn't we have to find out first if there was someone there who was willing to talk to us?' asked Holly. 'Otherwise there wouldn't be any point in going. There might not be anything to see.'

Abby turned to Kaitlin. 'Can I take the leaflet to show to Mum?'

she asked. 'She could phone up and ask if they'd help us.'

Michelle smiled. 'I think we've decided what our secret project is now. I'll see what Dad says tonight, and it looks as if Abby's mum will help us, too. I think we should start writing a list of questions for the interviewing.'

The others agreed readily, and soon they were deep in discussion.

They did not notice the time passing until they heard the door open, and they all swung round to see who was there. It was Kaitlin's Auntie Jean.

'You're all very quiet,' she observed. 'I'm very grateful. I feel quite a lot better now I've had that sleep.'

Abby quickly shut her jotter.

'Ah,' said Auntie Jean, 'you're obviously very busy. Well, don't let me disturb you.' She looked at her watch. 'You've got nearly another hour before I have to go. I'll have a shower, and you can get on with your meeting.'

'Meeting.' Kaitlin liked the sound of that. The way her auntie had said it made her feel quite grown up.

By the time they had to part, they had drawn up a list of questions that more than filled a page of Abby's jotter.

'I can think of lots more,' said Holly. 'I'll write them all down at home.'

'We'd better get together again tomorrow,' Abby decided.

'I'll see if you can all come to my house,' Holly told them. 'I'll send a text this evening if it's going to be okay.'

Having received a text from Holly that evening, Abby, Kaitlin and Michelle arrived at her house promptly at two o'clock the following day.

Abby was clutching her pink jotter tightly to her chest.

'It's not going to get away from you, you know,' Michelle teased, pointing to the jotter.

'That's not why I'm holding it tightly,' Abby replied indignantly. 'It gives me a nice warm feeling inside because it's full of important things.'

'I know,' said Michelle. 'I feel the same way about mine, even though it doesn't have much in it yet.'

Kaitlin rang the bell, and Holly appeared straight away. She opened the door wide and beckoned them in.

'Come and say hello to my gran, and then we'll go upstairs to my room,' she instructed.

Abby had not met Holly's gran before, and when she did, she had quite a surprise. She knew only one of her own grans, and she had a face full of kindly wrinkles that was framed by curly white hair. Holly's gran had straight black hair, red lipstick and was wearing the kind of clothes that Abby's mum sometimes wore when she was going out in the evening. Abby realised that she had wrinkles, but the black hair and the lipstick made it look as if she would not have any, so you did not notice them at first.

When Holly's gran saw them, she jumped up from the sofa and gave each of them a hug and a kiss as Holly introduced them. 'Call me Maude,' she declared firmly. Kaitlin wondered if Maude was like this with everyone she met, but it felt nice anyway.

'Come and get me if there's anything you want,' said Maude expansively. Then she sat down again, and picked up a thick glossy magazine that lay on the sofa beside her. Michelle could see that it was *Marie-Claire*. Fleetingly she felt very puzzled, because her own gran only bought cross-stitch magazines.

Upstairs, Holly lay on her bed, propping her head up on one elbow. Before the others had arrived, she had arranged a beanbag, a dining chair and the wooden kitchen stool next to her bed. 'Sit down,' she directed. 'Any news yet?'

'I've got a bit,' Michelle replied. 'I talked to my dad.' She looked uncomfortable.

'What's the matter, Michelle?' asked Kaitlin kindly.

'I couldn't think of any way of asking him without telling him about our project,' Michelle admitted worriedly.

'What's wrong with that?' asked Holly. She could not work out why Michelle was uneasy.

'I hadn't asked you all if it was okay to tell him about it,' Michelle explained, 'and by the time I was talking to him, it was too late to ask you.'

'But you *had* to say,' Abby pointed out. 'Anyway, I had to when I was talking to Mum about the place on the leaflet.'

Michelle looked relieved.

'Tell us what he said,' Kaitlin urged.

Michelle became animated. 'Well, I was right. Dad *does* know someone. He's called Brian. He started up his dog training business this year, and he's got lots of business already. *And...*' Here she paused dramatically.

'And what?' Holly asked. 'Don't keep us in suspense.'

'Brian's got a friend who's helping to train guide dogs for the blind.'

'Wow!' exclaimed Kaitlin. 'Are we going to get to talk to them both? It would take our project a lot further than pet care, but I don't care.' She giggled. 'Care and care...'

'Dad's not promising anything yet,' Michelle told them, 'except that he's going to talk to Brian soon.'

Abby was sitting on the kitchen stool. Holly noticed that she had started to wriggle about.

'Is there something wrong with the stool?' she asked.

'No,' Abby replied. 'It's just that I'm desperate to tell you all my news. Michelle's news is really good, but I've got some as well.'

'I've finished mine,' said Michelle, 'so it's your turn now.'

Abby sat up very straight on the stool. 'Mum phoned the number on the leaflet last night,' she announced. 'She spoke to a really nice woman, and they had a long chat.'

By now Holly was leaning so far forward at the edge of her bed that she nearly fell off, and she had to grab at Kaitlin's knee to stop herself.

'Go on, Abby,' urged Kaitlin.

Abby took a deep breath. 'What they decided was that when you come to my house for a weekend, Mum will take us to see her for a *whole evening*.'

'Wow!' said Holly. 'We'll fill up most of our jotters with that.'

'We'd better not,' Michelle reminded her, 'there could be loads of stuff from Brian and his friend, too.'

Abby hugged herself. 'We've got such an exciting project, and no one at school knows what it is. They're going to get a big surprise when we go back after the holidays.'

Just then they heard Maude calling up the stairs, and Kaitlin swung round and opened the door.

'What is it, Gran?' shouted Holly.

'I've got something for you,' Maude called back.

'Okay, I'll come down.' Holly bounced off her bed and ran quickly down the stairs. She was soon back, carrying a tray with a large thermos jug and four glasses on it.

'We're in luck,' she informed them.

'What is it?' asked Abby curiously.

'It's a Gran Special,' replied Holly mysteriously. 'A Gran Smoothie,' she added cryptically. Carefully she poured a little of the contents of the jug into each glass and handed them round.

'I like smoothies,' said Kaitlin. 'You haven't given me a lot. Is there more?'

Holly smiled. 'There's loads more, but you'd better try it first. There's no smoothie like a Gran Smoothie.'

Kaitlin sipped from her glass. Holly was right. She had never tasted anything like this before. She savoured it, and then took a large mouthful. It was…

Abby and Michelle followed her example.

'It's… *stupendous!*' Michelle exclaimed. 'I've had loads of smoothies before, but nothing like this. Holly, what does she make it from?'

Abby had emptied her glass, and she held it out for more. 'Yes, what does she make it from?' she echoed.

Holly shared out the rest of the smoothie from the jug, and then perched on the edge of her bed, sipping meditatively from her glass.

'Why aren't you saying anything?' asked Kaitlin.

Holly laughed. 'There's nothing to tell you except that she

won't tell anyone.'

Kaitlin thought about this for a minute, and then said, 'I'm not surprised. I think that someone could make a lot of money if they copied it.'

After this they all fell silent as they savoured their treat.

When they had finished, Holly turned to Abby. 'Did your mum say anything yet about when we'll be at yours?'

'She's going to write proper invitations,' Abby replied proudly.

'That's nice, but for when?' asked Michelle.

'She's not completely sure yet, but she thinks it'll be for the weekend after next.'

Michelle bounced excitedly on the beanbag, but fell off backwards and jammed herself against the wall.

'Help!' she gasped in mock dismay.

Abby and Kaitlin grabbed an arm each and pulled her back on to the beanbag.

Abby went on. 'Mum says she'll invite you all for Friday night until Sunday night, and she'll take us to something nice on one of the days.'

The others stared at Abby.

'That's really really kind of her,' said Holly.

Kaitlin and Michelle nodded vigorously. 'We can help with the cooking and things,' they said together.

Suddenly Abby looked worried. 'Are you all free that weekend?' she asked.

'Now I'm back from our holiday away, there's not much happening at home,' Holly replied.

Kaitlin and Michelle agreed. 'The only thing that's happening is our project,' Kaitlin added.

'I've just thought of something,' said Holly suddenly. 'It's a pity the people in the food group can't meet my gran. She knows loads about food and where it all comes from. I think they'd learn a lot.' She giggled. 'But one thing they wouldn't learn is the secret recipe for the smoothie.' She was quiet for a moment, and then added, 'If I bump into Megan or Nicole, I might say something. I don't think I'll be seeing any of the others.'

'That leaves Cameron, Mark and Usman,' said Kaitlin. 'If we see one of them, shall we say something about it to them?'

'Better not,' decided Holly. 'I'll have to talk Gran round first. We were lucky to have her here today. She's usually so busy with her clients.'

'Clients?' said Kaitlin.

'Yes, she does beauty treatments for people. And it isn't just painting faces, you know,' Holly added importantly. 'Beauty comes from within. She does detox programmes and confidence-something-or-other as well.'

Michelle thought that when Holly said 'Beauty comes from within' she sounded as if she was quoting out of a book about one of those period dramas that her mum liked to watch on TV, but she said nothing. She was intrigued. There was a lot more to Maude than she could ever have imagined.

Two days later, Abby delivered her mother's invitations to her friends. Her mother had made a lovely job of them, and she felt very proud. The invitations were decorated with line drawings of different animals, and Abby was given a special pen filled with gold paint so that she could draw something on the envelopes. Abby had made a scrolly pattern all round the edges of the envelopes, back and front. Each invitation set out what they would be doing that weekend.

The trip to the pet-care place was to be on Saturday evening, and on Sunday morning, Michelle's dad's friend, Brian, was coming round to talk to them with his friend, who would tell them a bit about not only guide dogs for the blind, but also about hearing dogs for the deaf, and sniffer dogs for the police. This had been a surprise even to Abby. Once her mum had heard about Brian, she had found out from Michelle's dad how to contact him, and she had fixed the visit up as a special surprise.

What no one knew then was that Brian and his friend were making plans to arrange with Abby's mum that after coming to the house, they would take everyone for a visit to another dog trainer.

Chapter Four – The Exercise Project

Sam's dad, Bruce, had arranged the first exercise group meeting at the local sports centre where he was a member.

Shona, Emma, Stephen and Shannon had arrived more than half an hour early, as they could not wait to get started. They flopped down on the closely mown grass at the front of the building. Shannon had wanted to bring her new bike to show to the others, but in the end had decided not to, as she was not sure if there would be anywhere safe to leave it.

'I asked Mum and Dad about fundraising,' said Shona. 'They weren't keen at first, and started asking me loads of questions about what we were planning to do. But when I told them that Sam's dad was going to be in charge of us, they agreed straight away.'

Stephen, Shannon and Emma were very pleased to hear this.

'I want to raise money for "Sightsavers",' Emma announced.

'What's that?' asked Stephen.

'It's really good,' Emma replied. 'They put antibiotic ointment on people's eyes in Africa when they get infected. If they don't get that treatment, a lot of them go blind.'

'That's terrible!' exclaimed Shannon, aghast. 'I hope I can use my new bike to help to get money for the antibiotic. I'll pedal as fast as I can.' She lay on her back and pedalled her feet quickly in the air.

Just then, Stephen spotted Sam and his dad walking up the access road.

'Here they are at last,' he said.

Shona consulted her watch. 'Actually, they're ten minutes early,' she corrected him.

Sam jogged the last few hundred yards, and flopped down on the grass beside them, panting.

31

'Hello everyone,' Bruce greeted them as he came closer. 'This is what I like to see – everyone keen and ready to go. Let's get down to business.' He sat on the grass with them. 'Now, if we're to go about this properly, the first thing is to teach you a safe warm-up routine.'

'I don't need that,' Shannon objected. 'When I've got my bike, I can jump on and whizz off straight away.' Again she lay on her back, and pedalled her feet in the air.

'I'm sure you can,' Bruce acknowledged kindly, 'but it's important that you learn safe ways of going about strenuous exercise. It's best to practise using them now, and you'll definitely need them when you're older, or you'll run the risk of ending up with a pulled muscle, or something worse. If you watch how the top footballers do things, or ballet dancers and athletes, you'll see that they all do warm-up routines.'

Shannon sat up and leaned forward attentively. 'Okay,' she said eagerly. 'I'm ready.' Then she covered her face with her hands. 'Oh no!'

'What's the matter?' asked Emma, concerned.

Shannon looked very upset. 'I should have brought my special blue jotter that Miss Fairhurst gave me.'

'Don't worry, Shannon, you can share mine for now,' Shona consoled her. She opened the bag she had brought, and took it out.

'That's kind of you,' Bruce commented, 'but you won't need jotters today. I've got some sheets here that show you everything.' He took a folder out of his sports bag and produced some sheets showing puppet-like figures in various postures, underneath each of which was some writing. 'I'll go through the first part of this programme with you today, and you can practise at home. I'll demonstrate some more when we get together again. Now, everyone stand up and we'll make a start.'

They all jumped to their feet. The next twenty minutes were spent learning a lot of new things, some of which they found quite challenging.

When eventually Bruce looked at his watch, he said, 'You've all done very well indeed, but that's enough for today.'

'But I want to do more,' Shannon burst out. 'I've got to get really really fit, so I can get money for Sightsavers.' She started to cry.

Bruce looked concerned. 'Let's all sit down and have a chat,' he directed gently. Once they were settled, he asked, 'Now what's all this about money?'

'We wanted to see if we could do something that meant we could get sponsors so that we can raise money for charity,' Shona explained. 'My mum and dad would help with the money bit.'

'I was telling everyone about Sightsavers,' said Emma.

Shannon blew her nose loudly and added, 'And I want to help the poor people in Africa that might go blind if they don't get antibiotic.'

Stephen nodded vigorously. 'Me too.'

'I'm very glad to hear all this,' Bruce replied. 'I've a lot of respect for what you want to do, and I'll do my best to help. But the first thing you must learn is that in order to help other people properly, you've got to make sure you're all right yourselves. It wouldn't be much good if you tried to save other people by dashing about, but ending up hurting yourselves or collapsing.'

Sam giggled. 'Then we'd need people to help *us*.'

His father nodded. 'Although it's fine to accept help when you need it, it's important to do things in the way that minimises risk. We want to avoid accidents or severe exhaustion.'

Shannon gazed at Bruce. She liked the way that he explained things, and she knew she could trust him to help them. They had all known Sam's dad since they started school, as he often helped with the after-school club. She could not remember what his main job was, but she knew he started work very early in the mornings, so he finished soon after lunch and could do sports after that.

Bruce continued. 'The things I've shown you today are all things you can try out at home. Read the instructions on the sheet carefully, and you can't go wrong. They tell you how many times to do each exercise, and how to spread exercise through each day.'

'When can we learn the next bit of the programme?' asked Shannon eagerly.

Bruce thought for a moment. 'I think the best thing would be for us to meet here again soon to see how things are going.'

'Tomorrow?' asked Stephen.

'That would be a bit soon,' Bruce replied. 'How about the day after? Same time, same place. By then you'll have had a reasonable amount of time to try out what you've learned already.' He checked his watch and jumped to his feet. 'Time for my game of squash now. Hope to see you all the day after tomorrow.' He disappeared through the doors into the sports centre.

'I feel all floppy,' Emma announced, 'and it's a good feeling.'

'Let's do some more exercises now!' said Shannon. She stood up and started to run on the spot.

'I'm not ready yet,' Shona told her. 'I'd like to do some more today, but later. In any case, I've got to go to the library to renew Mum's books.'

Shannon stopped running. 'I could come as well,' she offered.

'Why don't we meet here again tomorrow?' Stephen suggested.

'But Bruce won't be here,' Emma objected.

'That doesn't mean that we can't practise our exercises together,' Stephen pointed out.

'Okay,' agreed Emma.

The others thought that this was a good idea, and they arranged to meet at the same time.

Emma turned to Shona and Shannon. 'Can I come to the library, too?'

Shona nodded, and the three set off together.

Stephen surprised Sam by saying, 'Fancy a run round the park?'

'Okay.'

'I'm going home for some shorts and a T-shirt,' said Stephen, and he dashed off, calling over his shoulder, 'See you at the main gates.'

Half an hour later they were at the gates, ready to start.

'My dad sometimes jogs to work,' Stephen commented as they

set off.

Sam was impressed, and said so.

By this time, Shannon, Shona and Emma had arrived at the library, and Shona had handed in her mum's books.

'I want to look for a book on exercise,' Shannon announced. She looked round the library, spotted a section on sports, and went to examine the books there.

'I'm going to ask the librarian about health and fitness,' Emma whispered to Shona.

'That's a good idea,' Shona whispered back. 'I think we're allowed to look at those books while we're here, but we can't borrow them. You've got to have a ticket like Mum's before you can.'

The librarian was very helpful, and she took them across to three shelves of books in the non-fiction section of the main library.

'There may be a few books to look at in the children's section as well,' she said quietly. 'I'll go and check the catalogue.'

Shona and Emma were soon engrossed.

After a while, Shona nudged Emma. 'Look at this one,' she said in a low voice. 'It's about yoga. It's really interesting.'

Emma replaced a slim book on the shelf. 'Let's sit at a table and read some of it together,' she suggested.

Minutes later, they were studying a section on breathing. 'I hadn't thought about breathing before,' Shona whispered. 'I thought it was something that just happened.'

Shannon came to join them. 'I can't find anything in the sports section that I want to read,' she said mournfully. 'What have you got?'

'Shush,' whispered Emma and Shona together. They pointed to their book, and Shannon looked over their shoulders and read for a while.

They did not notice the librarian until she spoke to them, and they all jumped.

'Sorry to startle you,' she said, 'but this book has just been returned for the children's section. It might interest you.' She put it on the table and returned to her desk.

The following day, the group assembled outside the sports centre.

Sam took charge. 'I'll be Dad,' he said confidently.

Shannon pulled a face. 'But you're not.'

'I'd rather we just did the exercises together without a leader,' said Stephen.

'Okay,' Sam agreed amiably.

They worked hard, and then lay on the grass together.

'I've got an idea,' Stephen announced.

'What sort of idea?' asked Shannon curiously.

'Yes, what sort of idea?' the others echoed.

'About what we might do for being sponsored,' Stephen explained.

The others sat up, and Stephen continued.

'I thought we might do a sort of triathlon thing, except there would be five things, and each of us would do one of the things – one at a time.'

'That's a really cool idea,' said Shannon as she imagined herself pedalling her bike as fast as she could, with everyone cheering her on.

'Dad could have his stopwatch,' Sam suggested, 'so we could give the sponsors a detailed report.'

'Hey, that's good,' Emma approved.

Sam continued. 'He could time us to do fifteen minutes each.'

Shona looked anxious. 'What if I was exhausted before I'd done my fifteen minutes?' she asked.

'That's what we're doing all this warming up for,' Sam explained. 'After we're good at warming up, Dad can help us to build up our stamina.'

Shona still looked anxious. 'I'd be so embarrassed if I didn't finish my fifteen minutes.'

'We could have it as ten minutes each,' Stephen suggested.

Shona relaxed. 'Let's do that,' she agreed. Then she added hastily, 'But if I build up my stamina and want to do fifteen minutes, we could change it.'

The others were satisfied with this plan, and they went on to discuss what each of them would be doing.

'I'll be riding my bike, of course,' Shannon began.

'And I'll be running,' said Stephen.

Sam looked thoughtful. 'I think I'll talk to Dad about mine,' he decided.

'I know what I want to do,' said Emma, 'but it might not fit in.'

'What is it?' asked Sam. 'Dad's bound to help.'

'Swimming,' replied Emma. 'Back crawl.'

'Yes, you've got to do that,' Shona encouraged. 'You're really good at it. We could start our group triathlon thing at the swimming pool, and then Stephen could dash out of the building and run round the park...'

Shannon butted in. 'And then I can set off on my bike.'

Emma looked at Shona. 'You're good at swimming, too. Could you do something in the pool after me?'

Sam was excited. 'I can't wait to tell Dad about all this when I see him later.'

'We should all tell him tomorrow,' Stephen told him firmly.

'I can't wait,' said Sam flatly.

'You've *got* to,' Shannon insisted. 'It's not just your project, it's *ours.*'

Sam had a look of rebellion on his face, but he agreed, albeit reluctantly.

'There's something that's bothering me,' said Emma. 'We can't call it a group triathlon, because there are going to be five things in it, not three.'

'I know!' said Shona brightly. 'My mum told me that when someone has five babies, they're called quins, so we can call our five thing a quintathlon.'

Stephen was standing quietly, lost in thought.

'What is it, Stephen?' asked Emma.

'I think the word we're looking for is "pentathlon".'

'I think so, too,' agreed Sam. 'I can ask Dad about that tonight without telling him why I need to know.'

The others agreed. They would tell Bruce everything tomorrow. And when the plan was finalised, Shona's mum and dad would start to help with sponsoring...

Chapter Five – The Foods Project

It was nearly three weeks into the summer holiday before Mark, Usman, Cameron, Megan and Nicole could meet to begin their project. Megan and her dad had obtained a large map of the world, and once he had checked its dimensions, her dad made a lovely board with a cork surface so that not only could they fix the map on to it easily, but also they could put pins in wherever necessary. They had bought packs of pins with brightly coloured heads of different colours, ready for when Megan and her friends could make a start.

Several times Megan had gone shopping for groceries with her mum, and each time she had taken her green jotter with her. She liked to help her mum, but now she always spent time scrutinising the labels of food products as well. She found this very interesting, and made several lists in her jotter. Most of the labels indicated only the country of origin, but as they had discussed in class, she found plenty where the region and grower were also named.

She listed locally grown produce on one page of her jotter, foods from the rest of the UK on another, foods from Europe on another, and then used another few pages for the rest of the world. She had heard so many people talking about how it was good to buy local produce, and a recent programme that she had seen on TV explained exactly why. She had not thought much before about food being transported, but watching the programme had left her thinking a lot about how far food travelled, and how much fuel was used up in transporting it. And it was not just the fuel costs that counted. There was so much talk now about carbon footprints, and how when fuel was burned it added to the problems of global warming. It was all very worrying. She wished that she understood more about it all, but she trusted that there were people somewhere who were trying to work out what was best to do. Meanwhile she was determined to do her best to help by not buying food that had travelled a long way.

She knew that it was also important to think about the freshness of the food. She had heard that the longer fresh food had to travel, the less nutritious it was, even if it was refrigerated.

Several years earlier, her dad had turned their large garage into a big workshop, leaving his car out on the drive. Now he hung the map on one wall of the workshop, and suggested that she invited her friends round to share the information that they had gathered so far. Megan was very happy with this idea, and soon arranged an evening when everyone could come. Cameron did not mind that this meeting was not going to be at his house after all.

That afternoon, Megan and her mum made some oat biscuits that she could hand round, and they bought some fizzy water that was flavoured with ginger. Megan collected five folding chairs from the shed, and put them in the workshop, ready for her friends to arrive.

Mark and Nicole came first, both carrying their jotters.

'I've got lists and lists of foods in my jotter,' said Nicole happily.

'So have I,' Mark joined in.

Megan laughed. 'I have, too.'

'I wonder what the others have done,' said Mark.

Nicole looked at her watch. 'It's nearly seven. I hope they come soon.'

'Come into Dad's workshop and sit down,' Megan suggested. 'I'll show you the map, and we could start putting some of the coloured pins in it.'

'Hey, this is good!' exclaimed Mark as he saw the map. 'It's pretty big.'

'Yes, Dad and I were pleased with it. We thought it was best to have plenty of room on it,' Megan told him.

'Shouldn't we wait for the others?' asked Nicole uncertainly. 'I don't want them to feel left out.'

'I suppose we could wait for a while,' Mark decided. 'But that doesn't stop us from looking at where some of the places are on the map.'

'Dad said we could use his atlas if we got stuck,' said Megan. 'If we're not sure where somewhere is, we can look up place names in the index.'

Mark smiled. 'That's great.'

The three were soon absorbed in matching some of the place names to areas on the map, and Megan jumped when she heard the side door of the workshop open. She spun round and saw Usman and Cameron there.

'Oh, it's you!' she exclaimed.

'Sorry we're late,' said Usman. 'Cameron came round, and I was so busy getting some things together that I made us both late.' He was carrying a small cardboard box.

'What's in there?' asked Nicole curiously.

'You'll see in a minute,' said Usman casually. 'Dad does a lot of interesting cooking, and he uses lots of different things. He gave me some to bring along.'

'Mm,' said Megan thoughtfully. 'If they're spices, they don't weigh much. That means it's okay to eat them.'

'What do you mean?' asked Nicole.

'I think most of them are grown in countries a long way away,' Megan began.

'So they have to travel a long way to get here,' Mark added.

'But because they don't weigh much, they don't have to use up much fuel to get them here,' Cameron finished.

'I want to put some pins in,' said Megan suddenly. 'I've waited and waited for ages until you could all come round.'

'Okay,' replied Mark. 'How shall we do it?'

'We could have one colour of pin for meat, one for vegetables, one for fruit...' Nicole suggested.

'That's a good idea, but I think it might get a bit complicated,' replied Megan. 'How about starting off with a colour each, and putting in ten pins each?'

The others agreed, and they were soon busily consulting their jotters, the map, and sometimes the atlas.

When they had finished, they stood back and admired the effect.

'They're spread all over the place,' Cameron observed. 'And I've got plenty more foods listed in my jotter.'

'I've learned quite a lot just doing my ten pins,' said Mark, 'and I'd like to find out what all the other pins are for.'

'I want to do that, too,' Nicole agreed.

They took it in turns to talk about the foods that they had chosen for the map.

After that, Megan turned to Usman. 'Can you show us what's in your box now?'

'Okay,' he replied.

'Oh!' exclaimed Megan. 'I forgot about the refreshments. Let's have them first.'

She hurried out of the workshop, and soon came back with a round tin and some plates.

'Hand the biscuits round,' she directed, 'and I'll get the drinks.'

When she returned, Usman had opened his box and was holding out a small jar to Mark.

'Hey!' she said crossly. 'You were supposed to wait for me.'

Usman placated her by saying, 'I'll give you the next one.'

She handed the drinks round and Usman passed a small plastic container to her.

'I took the labels off everything because you're all supposed to guess what they are,' he explained.

'It looks like dried leaves in this one,' Megan said.

'And this is a powder,' added Mark, shaking the jar that Usman had given to him. 'But I haven't a clue what it is.'

'Let me see,' said Nicole. 'Mm… I've seen something like this at my auntie's boyfriend's house. He's interested in cookery as well. Usman, is it wasabi powder?'

'Yes, it is,' Usman replied.

'I thought so,' said Nicole. 'My auntie's boyfriend put it on his steak. But where does it come from?'

Cameron smirked. 'The supermarket, of course.'

Nicole scowled at him. 'Stop spoiling this.'

Cameron apologised. 'Sorry. I was just teasing.'

'Well, *don't*,' said Nicole severely.

'The label said it was from Japan,' Usman told them.

'Put a pin in the map for it,' Megan instructed. 'We haven't got anything in Japan yet.'

Usman inserted a pin in Hokkaido, and then turned back to Megan. 'You're right about the stuff in the container I gave to you. It is definitely dried leaves.'

'Even though they're dried, they look quite greenish,' Megan commented as she handed the container to Cameron.

No one had any ideas about what the leaves were, so Usman had to tell them.

'They are Kaffir lime leaves, and they're from Thailand.'

'What on earth are they used for?' asked Nicole.

'I'll have to ask Dad,' Usman admitted.

'Well, at least put a pin in the map,' said Megan.

Usman looked uncomfortable. 'Er... I'm not sure where Thailand is.'

Cameron surprised them all by jumping to his feet. He pointed confidently at the map. 'It's here. It's in the big bit that sticks down from China, to the right – I mean the east – of India.' He stuck a pin in and sat down again.

The others were impressed.

'How did you know that?' asked Mark.

'Well, Vietnam is next to it,' Cameron replied. 'Dad's told me quite a lot about the war in Vietnam, and he showed me where it was.' He leaned over and looked into Usman's box. 'Hey!' he exclaimed. 'Here's some tamarind. I once had some of that.' He picked it up, but Usman took it from him and handed it to Nicole.

'It looks a bit like a pack of cooking dates,' she remarked, 'but the label has funny writing on it.'

'Dad told me we could try some,' Usman informed everyone.

Nicole wrinkled up her nose. 'I'm not sure that I want to.'

'You can have another of my oat biscuits,' said Megan as she quickly passed the plate across to her. 'Usman, where is the tamarind from?'

'That's from Thailand, too,' he replied. He picked two more containers from his box and handed them to Cameron to pass round.

'I think I know what these are,' said Nicole immediately. 'Can I smell them?'

Usman nodded.

Nicole opened the packs and breathed deeply from each in turn.

'Vanilla pods and cinnamon sticks,' she pronounced triumphantly.

'You're right,' Usman told her. 'But does anyone know where they are from?'

Mark looked thoughtful. 'I bet they've come from somewhere in that bit where Thailand is,' he began.

Usman looked uncomfortable again. 'I've only got the names of the countries,' he admitted. 'I didn't have time to look to see where they are.'

Mark went to the map and looked at Thailand. 'Tell us where they're from, and I'll find the places.'

'Cinnamon sticks from Sri Lanka and vanilla pods from Indonesia,' Usman replied.

'Indonesia is these islands quite a bit south of Thailand,' Mark reported briskly. 'Now, where's Sri Lanka...'

'I can look it up in the atlas,' Megan offered.

'No thanks,' replied Mark. 'I want to find it.'

The others gave him a few minutes for his search.

'Got it now!' he declared. 'It's a big island east of the tip of India.'

It was nearly ten o'clock by the time they had finished talking, and Megan's dad came to tell them that he would see them all home safely.

'I'll be fine,' said Usman, flexing his muscles.

'I'm sure you would be,' replied Megan's dad, 'but I'd like to see you home anyway.'

They were on their way down the road together when they bumped into Holly and her dad, who were taking a dog for a walk.

'Hi!' called Megan. 'Whose dog is that?'

'It's Mr Bromley's from down our road,' Holly explained. 'You can give him a pat. He's really gentle. His name is Ruff. Mr Bromley has had to spend a night in hospital, so we said we would help out with Ruff.' She nearly started talking about the pet-care project, but managed to stop herself in time. Instead she asked, 'How's your food project going?'

'We've had a meeting this evening,' Megan explained. 'Me and Dad are taking everyone home now.'

They were about to part when Holly remembered about her gran. 'Oh,' she said, 'I was going to mention to you about my gran. She's a beauty therapist, and she knows loads and loads about food.'

'Oh, thanks,' Mark replied. 'Do you think she'd talk to us about our project?'

'I think she might,' said Holly. 'The trouble is that she can be very busy, so she doesn't have much spare time. Shall I ask her?'

Everyone agreed to this, and Holly promised that she would speak to her as soon as she could.

Chapter Six – The World War Two Project

Jack had been looking forward to seeing Dylan, Ryan, Julie and Andrew. Although they had planned to keep in touch with one another over the holidays, it had not worked out that way. The weeks had flown past, and the promised texts had been few and far between.

It was now the final week of the holiday, and as arranged, they were going to meet every day at Jack's house to discuss their project. The weather was warm but showery, and Jack had persuaded his dad to put up the tent in the garden for their meeting place.

The others arrived after lunch, and Jack led them straight to the tent. They were impressed by the venue, and crowded in eagerly.

'Oh no!' said Julie. 'I forgot to bring my red jotter. I've brought some other things though.'

'I've forgotten, too,' added Andrew.

'It won't matter to begin with,' Jack told them. 'We've got all week.' He picked up his jotter and flapped it up and down. 'And I've got a huge amount of stuff I can tell you about.'

'Is that a fan or something?' asked Ryan cheekily.

Jack blew a raspberry at him, and then said, 'When I was away it was just like I'd hoped. I got a lot of information from Mum's uncle and aunt, and they had some friends nearby who invited me round. It was perfect.'

Dylan had brought what looked like an old briefcase with him.

'What's that for?' asked Julie.

'Dad lent it to me,' said Dylan proudly. 'He used it when he was young. And it's full of stuff we got when we went to the Imperial War Museum.'

'Wow!' exclaimed Ryan. 'Did you really get there in the end?'

'Yes,' Dylan replied. 'Dad took me away – just the two of us –

for a whole weekend. It was brilliant!' His face glowed as he thought of their trip.

'I haven't got all that much,' said Andrew. 'Dad's lent me some old medals that his dad got.'

'Let's have a look,' Dylan asked.

Andrew felt in the zip pockets of the lightweight jacket that he was wearing, and produced two medals out of each.

Dylan took one and studied it intently. 'This one looks like something I saw at the museum,' he pronounced.

'Dad's got some more things,' Andrew told them, 'but he didn't want me to take them out of the house. He said to tell you that you could come and see them if you want.'

'Of course we want to,' said Jack.

'Yes,' Julie agreed. 'Tell him.'

Andrew looked pleased. 'Okay. I'll talk to him and fix when you can come round.'

Ryan began to look miserable.

'What's the matter, Ryan?' asked Julie, concerned.

'I...' he mumbled. 'I haven't got anything.'

'You can share mine,' Julie offered immediately. 'I was just going to say that mine's all about what it was like for the women working in the factories and fields during the war. Gran's been helping me. There was stuff in her attic, and she's been talking to me about her mum, my great-granny, because she was a land girl.'

'I'm not interested in the women's stuff,' Ryan hissed at her.

Julie felt startled by his attitude, and a little hurt. Then she remembered how Miss Fairhurst had been kind to Chloe in class when she was rude, and she sensed that this was a time when Ryan, too, needed some extra kindness. She searched her mind for something else to say, but before she could think of something, he hung his head and began to speak.

'I wanted to do something with my dad, but he had to go away for work all summer. I didn't feel like doing it on my own.'

'Hey, Ryan,' said Dylan. 'I've got far too much in the briefcase to go through on my own, and I was really lucky that my dad was free to take me to the museum. How about we share some of this out between us?'

Ryan scowled. 'I don't...' he began, but his voice trailed off as he realised that everyone was trying to help him and wanted him to be a proper part of their project. 'Thanks,' he finished gratefully.

'It's going to take me ages and ages to sort out everything I've collected,' said Jack. 'I've got loads of notes, and I've got photos and other things.' He suddenly looked rather weary. 'It was good fun collecting it all, but I was hoping that everyone would sort through it together. Andrew and Ryan, can you help?'

Julie smiled to herself. Ryan was going to be okay, so now she could get on with telling them some of what she had learned.

'I was reading Gran's newspapers,' she began. She looked in her bag and took out a bulging envelope. 'And I found an article "Factory girls endured too much to do their bit for the war effort". It says that the conditions in the factories were awful and that they had to work from 7.30 in the morning to 6.30 at night for six days a week.'

'You mean that the women had a bad time at home while the men were fighting?' asked Ryan.

Julie nodded vigorously. 'They worked really really hard. There were women in the factories, and there were Lumber Jills and Land Girls. The Land Army had a timber corps...'

Andrew gaped at her. 'I thought the war was all about men shooting and bombing.'

Julie shook her head emphatically. 'And there's something else here,' she added, looking through her newspaper cuttings. 'Here it is... "Gardeners prepare to move into Prisoner of War camp".'

'What does it say?' asked Ryan, fascinated. He had forgotten his earlier misery and was now deeply involved.

Julie began to read the article for them:

Cultybraggan
A former prisoner-of-war camp in Perth and Kinross that held German prisoners could be turned into allotments. Cultybraggan

48

camp, built in 1939, held up to 4,000 prisoners during the Second World War, including Hitler's deputy, Rudolph Hess, held there for a night after his aircraft crash-landed in Scotland...

'Rudolph Hess!' echoed Jack incredulously.

'That's what it says,' Julie confirmed.

The others looked at each other.

'Wow!' said Dylan, and then Andrew and Ryan said 'Wow!' together.

Ryan glanced over his shoulder as if he was checking to see that he would not be overheard. Then he leaned forward and whispered, 'Maybe when Dad's not so busy he'll take me there.'

Julie shuddered. 'There were some really horrible people alive then. But I've been to Germany on holiday, and I met loads and loads of really nice people there.'

'Things change,' Andrew reflected. 'I expect in 1939 no one ever thought we could end up being friends with Germany.'

'I've been thinking,' said Jack slowly. 'When we've sorted through all the stuff I've got, I think we might let the whole class use it. I'd planned that we would keep it for our own work in P7 so that we would get better marks than the others, but I think it would be best to share so everyone can learn more.'

'I want to do that with mine,' Julie agreed.

'I'll ask Dad about all this stuff we got from the museum,' said Dylan.

'And I'll check with Dad about his things,' Andrew added. 'He wouldn't lend them just to us, but he might lend them to the school.'

Chapter Seven – The Surprise

It was the first day of term, and the new P7 filed into their classroom and sat down.

'There's no sign of a teacher,' Laura observed unnecessarily.

'I wonder what's going to happen,' said Diane.

Ryan sniggered. 'Nothing much by the look of it.'

Mark was sitting next to him, and he dug his elbow into Ryan's ribs.

'Yeow!' shouted Ryan.

Just then Mrs Molloy appeared in the doorway.

'Primary seven!' she said severely. 'I expect better behaviour from you than this. You must set a good example to the rest of the school.'

The whole class fell completely silent and everyone sat up very straight in their seats.

'That's better,' said Mrs Molloy. 'Now, I have come to introduce you to your teacher for this year.' She turned round and beckoned to someone who was out of sight of the class. She turned back to the class and smiled. 'I believe you will all remember Miss Fairhurst.'

'Miss Fairhurst!' exclaimed the whole class together.

Miss Fairhurst came into the room and beamed at them. 'Yes, I'm joining the school for the whole of this year, and I am to be your class teacher,' she informed them. 'And first I'm looking forward to a full report about the summer.'

For other titles from Augur Press
please visit

www.augurpress.com

Tracy by Mirabelle Maslin

ISBN 0-9549551-0-2　£6.95

Tracy is twelve. A change in holiday plans means she spends her summer with her older cousin, Flora. Flora's mother, May, runs a bed and breakfast business. Tracy doesn't know quite what to expect...

A kaleidoscope of events and encounters leads Tracy and Flora into new experiences. Unfamiliar feelings and dilemmas abound. The interweaving of relationships with friends, their families and many others gradually opens up a world of creative possibilities for everyone.

Order from your local bookshop, amazon.co.uk or the augurpress website at www.augurpress.com

The Poetry Catchers
by The Pupils of Craigton Primary

ISBN 978-0-9549551-9-9   £7.99

Craigton Primary is an inner-city school in Glasgow, Scotland. It has over 200 poetry-mad pupils, and it is the first school in Glasgow to have its own poetry library! All of us have written a poem for this wonderful book. We have picked our favourite poems, and we hope that you enjoy reading them as much as we have enjoyed writing them. We have been inspired by Michael Rosen and our poetry-loving teacher, Mrs McCay. These poems include a selection of WACKY, WITTY and WONDERFUL thoughts, taken from our real-life experiences. Some of the poems will bring a tear to your eye, and others will make you cry with laughter. Why don't you open the book and see what's inside?

Order from your local bookshop, amazon.co.uk or the augurpress website at www.augurpress.com